Leap Back Home to Me

LAUREN THOMPSON

illustrated by
MATTHEW CORDELL

Margaret K. McElderry Books
New York • London • Toronto • Sydney

Leap frog over the ladybug.

Leap frog over the bee.

Leap frog over the tickly clover,

then leap back home to me!

Leap frog over the daisies.

Leap frog over the creek.

Leap frog over the splashing beavers,

then leap back home to me!

Leap frog over the owl's nest.
Leap frog over the trees.

Leap frog over the rocky hilltop,

then leap back home to me!

Leap frog over the mountains.

Leap frog over the sea.

Leap frog over the roaming clouds,

then leap frog back to me!

Leap frog over the sun.

Leap frog as high as you please.

Leap frog out to the farthest stars . . .

. . .when you leap home, here I'll be.

For Kevin
—L. T.

For Julie and Romy
—M. C.

MARGARET K. McELDERRY BOOKS • An imprint of Simon & Schuster Children's Publishing Division • 1230 Avenue of the Americas, New York, New York 10020 • Text copyright © 2011 by Lauren Thompson • Illustrations copyright © 2011 by Matthew Cordell • All rights reserved, including the right of reproduction in whole or in part in any form. • MARGARET K. McELDERRY BOOKS is a trademark of Simon & Schuster, Inc. • For information about special discounts for bulk purchases, please contact Simon & Schuster Special Sales at 1-866-506-1949 or business@simonandschuster.com. • The Simon & Schuster Speakers Bureau can bring authors to your live event. For more information or to book an event, contact the Simon & Schuster Speakers Bureau at 1-866-248-3049 or visit our website at www.simonspeakers.com. • Book design by Lauren Rille • The text for this book is set in ITC Esprit • The illustrations for this book are rendered in pen and ink with watercolor. • Manufactured in China • 0211 SCP • 10 9 8 7 6 5 4 3 2 1 • Library of Congress Cataloging-in-Publication Data • Thompson, Lauren. • Leap back home to me / Lauren Thompson ; illustrated by Matthew Cordell.—1st ed. • p. cm. • Summary: A little frog makes increasingly bold leaps out into the world, and then comes back to his mother after each excursion. • ISBN 978-1-4169-0664-3 (hc) • [1. Stories in rhyme. 2. Frogs—Fiction. 3. Mother and child—Fiction.] I. Cordell, Matthew, 1975– ill. II. Title. • PZ8.3.T32522Le 2011 • [E]—dc22 • 2009053708

FIRST
EDITION

E   Thompson, Lauren,
THOMPSON   1962-

           Leap back home to
           me.

$15.99

DATE			